To my double agents:
Caroline Walsh and Rebecca Watson—K. G.

To Lucy Napper—N. S.

Library of Congress Cataloging-in-Publication Data:
Gray, Kes.
006 and a half / Kes Gray and Nick Sharratt.
p. cm.
Summary: Daisy's plan to become a spy falls apart when no one
understands her spy language.
ISBN-13: 978-0-8109-1719-4
ISBN-10: 0-8109-1719-X
[1. Spies—Fiction. 2. Mothers and daughters—Fiction.]
I. Sharratt, Nick, ill. II. Title. III. Title: Double oh six and a half.
IV. Title: Oh oh six and a half.
PZ7.G77928Aab 2007
[E]—dc22
2006027478

Book design by Vivian Cheng

First published in 2006 by The Bodley Head, an imprint of Random House U.K.

Published in 2007 by Abrams Books for Young Readers, an imprint of Harry N. Abrams, Inc.

Printed and bound in Singapore
10 9 8 7 6 5 4 3 2 1

harry n. abrams, inc.
a subsidiary of La Martinière Groupe

115 West 18th Street
New York, NY 10011
www.hnabooks.com

006 and a Half

Kes Gray & Nick Sharratt

ABRAMS BOOKS FOR YOUNG READERS
NEW YORK

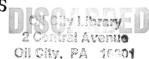

Daisy made up her mind. She wasn't going to be a girl anymore. She was going to be a spy.

She drew a spy's mustache on her top lip with a black felt-tip pen.

She found some dark glasses in a drawer.

She found some secret spy gadgets in her mom's bedroom. All she had to do now was speak in code. (Code is a special spy language that only spies understand. Daisy had seen it used in spy movies; now this time it was for real.)

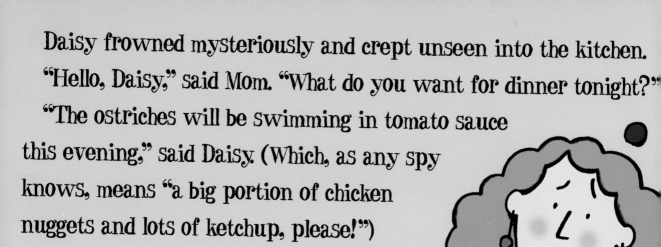

Daisy frowned mysteriously and crept unseen into the kitchen.
"Hello, Daisy," said Mom. "What do you want for dinner tonight?"
"The ostriches will be swimming in tomato sauce
this evening," said Daisy. (Which, as any spy
knows, means "a big portion of chicken
nuggets and lots of ketchup, please!")

Daisy's mom stared at Daisy and scratched her head.

"Why are you speaking in silly words?" asked Daisy's mom.

"They're not silly words," whispered Daisy mysteriously. "It's secret spy language. And my name isn't Daisy anymore. It's 006 and a Half."

"And what are you intending to do with my hairbrush, 006 and a Half?" asked Daisy's mom.

"It's not a hairbrush. It's my secret spy telephone," said Daisy.

"And where are you going with my perfume bottle?" asked Daisy's mom.

"It's not your perfume bottle," said Daisy. "It's my invisible ink."

"And would I be wrong in thinking that is my hairdryer?" asked Daisy's mom.

"Yes," whispered Daisy. "It's not a hairdryer. It's my secret baddie zapper."

Daisy's mom shook her head and went to find the ironing board.

006 and a Half slipped invisibly into the backyard.
"Hello, Daisy," said her neighbor. "How are you today?"
"Good afternoon, Agent Goldfish," said Daisy. "Are your
fins green or purple today?" (Which, as any spy
knows, means "I'm fine, thanks, Mrs. Pike.
How are you?")

Mrs. Pike stared strangely at Daisy and
went to mow her lawn.

Daisy slipped invisibly across the yard and went to give an important message to Mrs. Pike's cat.

"Meet me by the Golden Palace," she whispered. "And bring your furry overcoat." (Which, as any spy knows, means "Hello, Tiptoes, why don't you come and sit by the shed? I want to pet you.")

Tiptoes took one look at Daisy's hairdryer
and skedaddled over the wall.

Daisy dabbed on some invisible ink and peeped out of the gate. "No one will be able to see me now," she said with a smile.

"Hello, Daisy," said her best friend, Gabby. "Can you come out to play?"

"The laundry basket is full and the big busy beaver has many clothes to fold," Daisy said. (Which, as any spy knows, means "Hi, Gabby! I'll just ask my mom. She's doing the ironing.")

But Gabby gave Daisy a very strange look and
went to find someone else to play with.

Daisy took off her glasses and walked miserably back indoors.

"What's the matter, 006 and a Half?" asked her mom.
"Aren't you playing spies anymore?"

"No, I'm not." Daisy sighed. "No one understands my spy language. They just look at me as though I'm silly."

Daisy's mom stopped ironing and put her arm around Daisy's shoulders.

"That must be because they're not real spies," whispered her mom.

"If they were, they would understand everything you are saying."

Daisy trudged into the living room and slumped onto the sofa. "Well, they don't understand what I'm saying. There aren't any real spies around here, no one understands me, and I'm not being a spy anymore. Being a spy is stupid," she grumbled.

Daisy was just about to turn on the TV when a mysterious-looking stranger with a purple mustache and beard poked his head around the door. He had dark glasses on, just like Daisy's.

"Pssst," whispered the stranger in a deep, mysterious voice. "Have you seen 006 and a Half anywhere?"

Daisy stared back at the stranger in surprise. She quickly put her dark glasses on again and sat up straight.

"Yes, I have seen 006 and a Half!" She nodded. "That's me! I am 006 and a Half!"

"That is good news," whispered the stranger, "because my name is 0035 and a Half. I am a real spy, too!"

"The colored sprinkles will be meeting with the chocolate bar on the vanilla ice cream at dinnertime," whispered 0035 and a Half. "And the crunchy cream cookies and lemonade will be meeting under the big yellow comforter when the clock strikes twelve," continued the mysterious stranger.

006 and a Half frowned for a moment and clapped her hands excitedly. "Ooh goody! I know what that means!"

"We're having my favorite dessert for dinner and then a midnight feast in your bed tonight! I'll bring my comic and my flashlight, too!"

Which, as anybody knows, means "Thanks, Mom. You're the best spy in the world!"